HOW WILL THE
EASTER BUNNY
KNOW?

HOW WILL THE EASTER BUNNY KNOW?

Kay Winters

illustrated by **Martha Weston**

A Yearling First Choice Chapter Book

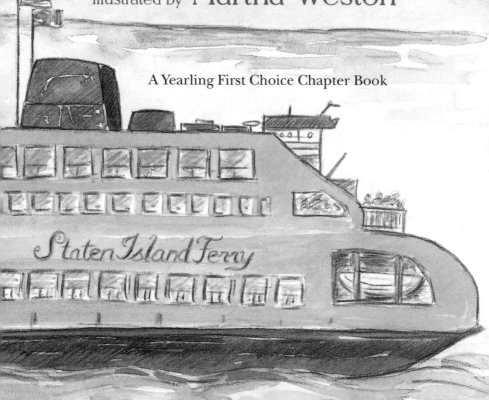

To John Coronati and his nephew, Matthew
—K.W.

To Anna and Gary
—M.W.

Published by
Bantam Doubleday Dell Publishing Group, Inc.
1540 Broadway
New York, New York 10036

Library of Congress Cataloging-in-Publication Data
Winters, Kay.
    How will the Easter bunny know? / Kay Winters ; illustrated by Martha Weston.
        p. cm.
    Summary: Mike, who will be spending Easter at his grandmother's
apartment, worries that the Easter Bunny will not know where to find him.
    ISBN 0-385-32596-7 (hardcover). —ISBN 0-440-41499-7 (pbk.)
    [1. Easter—Fiction.   2. Grandmothers—Fiction.]   I. Weston, Martha, ill.
II. Title.
PZ7.W7675Ho   1999
[E] —dc21   97-28798
                                                                      CIP
                                                                       AC

Visit us on the Web! www.bdd.com
Educators and librarians, visit the BDD Teacher's Resource Center at
www.bdd.com teachers

Hardcover: The trademark Delacorte Press® is registered in the U.S. Patent and
Trademark Office and in other countries.
Paperback: The trademark Yearling® is registered in the U.S. Patent and
Trademark Office and in other countries.
The text of this book is set in 17-point Baskerville.
Book design by Trish Parcell Watts
Manufactured in the United States of America
March 1999
10 9 8 7 6 5 4 3 2 1

CONTENTS

1.
GOOD NEWS, BAD NEWS

"We're going to Grandma's for Easter!"
said Mike to his friend Tony.

"The one with the elevator?" said Tony.

"Yes!" said Mike. "I get to
push the buttons!"

"But she doesn't have any kids,"
said Tony.

"Just my mom!" Mike laughed.

"Too bad," Tony said.

"What's wrong?" Mike asked.

"The Easter Bunny only comes
to houses with kids," Tony said.
"No!" said Mike. "That can't be true!"
"It is," said Tony. "I saw it on television.
The Bunny has a list that tells
where kids live."

"So Grandma's house won't be
on the list," Mike said.
A bad feeling crept up his chest.
A fire engine flashed by.

9

The crossing guard
waved the boys across.
"You'll get to ride the elevator,"
said Tony.
"So what?" said Mike.
"You'll get the goodies!"

The boys walked up
the steps of Tony's building.
They rang the bell.
"If we go to Grandma's for Easter,"
said Mike,
"how will the Bunny know?"

2.
A PHONE CALL

The boys climbed four flights of stairs.

Tony's sister, Anna, opened the door.

She was talking on the phone.

"If we knew the Bunny's number,

we could call him," Mike said.

"We'll get Anna to help," said Tony.

When Anna hung up the phone,

Tony told her they needed

the Easter Bunny's number.

"You kids!" she said.

But she got out the phone book.

"Where should I look first?" she asked.

"Try *R*," said Mike.

"Nobody's named Rabbit," said Tony.

"How about *B*?" Mike said.

"'Bunn, Bunnell, Bunney!'" read Anna.

"And here's one that starts with *E*!"

"Good luck, boys!" said Anna,
and she went to her room.
Mike was so excited,
it was hard to dial.
"Excuse me," he said
when someone answered.
"Is this the Easter Bunny?"

"No, it's not!" a voice shouted.

"You're the sixth kid to call this week!"

Mike hung up in a hurry.

"How about a plane that drags a sign?"

said Tony, looking out the window.

"Planes fly everywhere.

The Bunny would be sure to see it."

"No," said Mike. "Costs too much.

But we could make signs."

Mike drew

himself at Grandma's with Mom,

two cats, and a big Easter basket.

Tony drew Mike

and his mom in the elevator.

The signs said MIKE AT GRANDMA'S.

Mike's mom came for him after work.
Mike showed her the signs
they had made.
"So the Bunny will know where I am,"
he said.
"What a good idea!" said Mom.
"You think of everything!"
Mike rolled up the signs to take home.

3.
A MAP

The next day Mike talked
to his friend Ryan.
"Are you going away for Easter?"
Mike asked.

"Oh, no!" said Ryan.
"We always stay home.
Wouldn't want to miss
my Easter basket!"
So it's true, Mike thought.

Mr. Jamal told Mike's class
they would be learning about maps.
He showed them a map of the United
States and a map of New York.
"Now we'll make a map of our room,"
said Mr. Jamal.

Mr. Jamal taught the children
how to draw pictures on the map
to show where things were.

Mike gave a thumbs-up to Tony.
A map. Great idea.
They could make a map
for the Bunny!

After school Mike and Tony
hurried to Tony's apartment.
"Grandma lives on Staten Island,"
said Mike. "You take a ferry
to go there."
Tony drew Mike's building.
He made an arrow to the ferryboat.
Mike drew the boat passing
the Statue of Liberty.
Then he drew Grandma's apartment.
He colored her door green.
"Now he'll find me," said Mike.
He grinned at Tony.
"But how will the Bunny *get* the map?"
asked Tony.

"Oh, no!" said Mike.

"I didn't think of that."

The bad feeling came back.

At home that night Mike worried.

He worried when he went to bed.

He worried when he woke up.

He worried when Mr. Jamal
taught take-aways.

He worried at lunch,
even though there was
chocolate pudding.

Mr. Jamal was always telling Mike,
"You are full of shiny ideas,"
and giving him a high five.
That's what he needed now.
A shiny idea.

4,
THE SHINY IDEA

The next day after school,

Mike spotted the post office.

"That's it!" he said.

"The post office?" said Tony.

"Sure," said Mike.

"The post office knows

where everyone lives.

We'll write a letter."

"And send the map," said Tony.

"I want to write too," said Tony.

"Put 'Dear Easter Bunny,'" said Mike.

"We'll make pictures

for the hard words."

Then he took the pen.

"I will be at Grandma's for Easter.

Take the ferry to Staten Island.

Grandma lives in the redbrick

apartment with the green door."

Mike printed his name.

Tony added, "I will be home.

Love, Tony."

Mike put the letter and map

in an envelope.

He wrote "E. Bunny" on the front.

Dear Bunny,
I will be at Grandma's for . Take the to S.I. .
Grandma lives in the red with the green door.
Mike
I WILL Be Home.
LOVE,
TONY
MAP
E. Bunny

When Mike's mom came,
he showed her the letter and the map.
She put her arm around him.
"Mr. Jamal is right," she said.
"You do have shiny ideas!"
She gave Mike a stamp from her purse.

On the way home,

Mike put the letter in the mailbox.

"I hope he gets it in time," Mike said.

5.
THE TRIP

The day before Easter,
Mike packed his backpack.
He was excited!
They were going to Grandma's!
And the Easter Bunny would know
he was there.

Just to be sure,
Mike taped one sign
to the fire escape
and another
to the front door.

At last! It was time for the ferry.
Mike and his mom
could see the city
as the ferry sailed away.

Tall buildings and small buildings
glittered in the afternoon sun.
Mike and his mom waved
as they passed the Statue of Liberty.

When the ferry pulled in,
Grandma was at the dock.
She gave Mike a big hug.
"Tomorrow's the big day!" she said.
"Yes!" said Mike. "Can't wait!
And the Easter Bunny knows
where I am.
I made him a map!"
"Clever boy!" said Grandma.

They took a cab to Grandma's.
When the driver dropped them off,
Mike stood on the sidewalk and stared.
The building was redbrick,
just the way he'd showed on his map,
but the door wasn't green.
It was bright blue!

"Like the new door?" said Grandma.

"They just painted it yesterday."

Mom squeezed Mike's hand.

"It looks pretty!" said Mom.

They rode up in the elevator.

But Mike didn't even care

about pressing the buttons.

He felt as if he was sliding down.

He could hardly eat any supper.
"A blue door," he said to his mom.
"There's no way the Bunny
will find me now.
I told him it was green. Twice!"

At bedtime Mom came to tuck Mike in.

"Don't worry," she said.

"The Bunny is clever.

I'm sure he'll find you."

And she gave Mike a kiss.

Mike tossed and turned.
He dreamed he was in a field
of rabbits.
They were hippety-hopping,
thumping, and jumping.
Mike was chasing them.
"Over here," he kept calling.
"Come this way!"

6.
THE BIG DAY

The next morning,
Mike didn't want to get up.
"Rise and shine,"
called Grandma. "Happy Easter!"
Mike rubbed his eyes.
He was afraid to look.

Mike sat up slowly.

He walked into the living room.

A stuffed white rabbit
in a blue vest sat on the couch.
Next to him was an Easter basket
jammed with jelly beans
and chocolate eggs.
There was a pot of tulips for Mom,
and daffodils for Grandma.
"He found me! He came!" cried Mike.

The rabbit was holding an envelope.

Mike read the letter aloud.

> *Dear Mike,*
>
> *Thank you for your letter.*
>
> *And the map.*
>
> *And for making all those signs.*
>
> *You forgot one thing.*
>
> *The Easter Bunny is MAGIC.*
>
> *I will find you wherever you go.*
>
> > *Love,*
> >
> > *E. B. Rabbit*

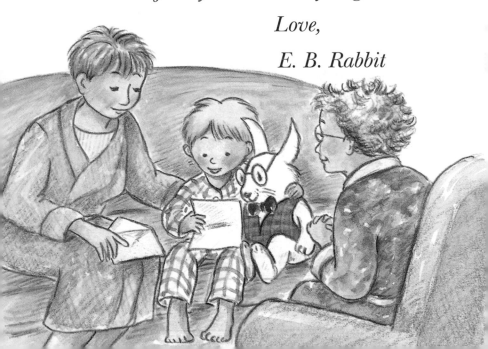

ABOUT THE AUTHOR

Kay Winters is the author of several books for children, including *Did You See What I Saw?: Poems About School, The Teeny Tiny Ghost,* and *Where Are the Bears?* She lives with her husband in Quakertown, Pennsylvania.

ABOUT THE ILLUSTRATOR

Martha Weston has illustrated more than forty children's books, including *Did You See What I Saw?* by Kay Winters. She lives in Fairfax, California, with her husband, two children, two cats, two fish, and a leopard gecko.